BRENDAN WENZEL

INSIDE CAT

chronicle books · san francisco

Inside Cat knows many windows,
finds a view wherever it goes.

Wanders.

Wonders.

Gazes.

Gapes.

Sees the world through many shapes.

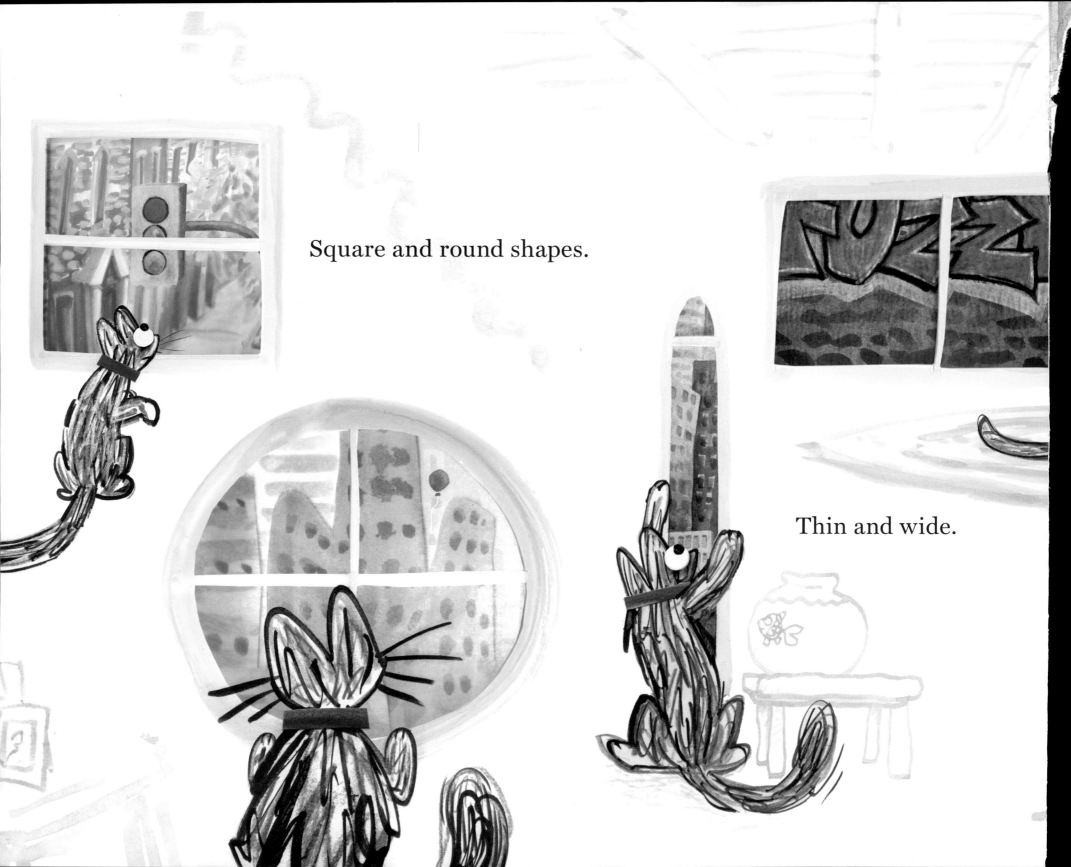

Square and round shapes.

Thin and wide.

Downward.

Upward.

Side by side.

View to view.
Floor to floor.

Knows the windows,
walls, and more.

Inside Cat knows many windows,
finds a view wherever it goes.

Wanders.

Wonders.

Stares.

Snacks.

Each scene through a pane of glass.

Glass all dusty.

Glass so streaky.

Glass gone gloomy.

Glass way freaky.

Glass all bubbly.

Glass got broken.

and glass wide open.

Glass that's blocked

View to view,
floor to floor.

Knows the windows,
walls, and more.

Inside Cat knows many windows,
finds a view wherever it goes.

Wanders.

Wonders.

Watches all things as they pass.

Laps.

Lingers.

Fluffy rats

and roaring flies.

Racing birds

and boats for mice.

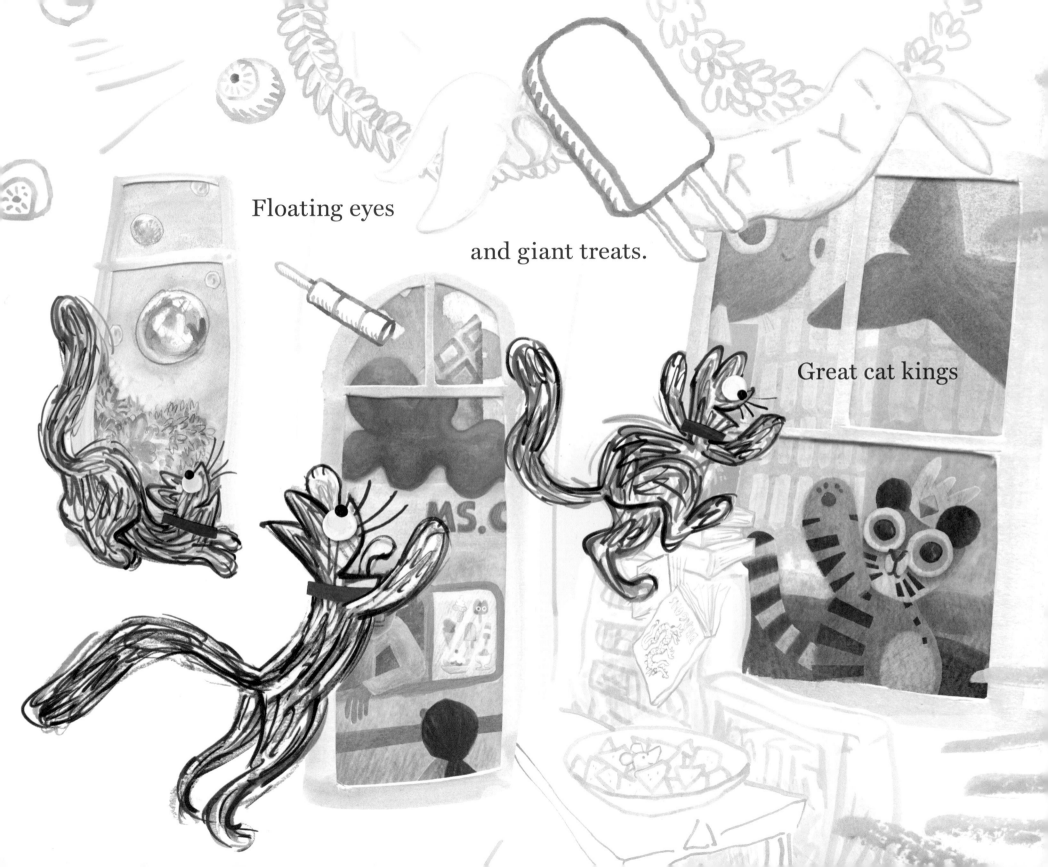

Floating eyes

and giant treats.

Great cat kings

View to view,
floor to floor.

Knows the windows,
world, and more.

and WILD BEASTS!

Inside Cat knows many windows,
finds a view wherever it goes.

Wonders.

Wanders.

Nibbles.

Naps.

Knows what's hiding in the gaps.

Knows who lives up in the clouds.

Knows who lives down in the ground.

Knows who is the fluffiest.

Knows who plays with all the kids.

Knows what blares.

Knows what smells.

Knows what speeds.

Knows what stares.

Knows what falls.

Knows what rises.

Inside Cat might know it ALL!

Every view and every floor.

All the windows, world, and more.

Top to bottom. Head to toe.

Nothing more for you to . . .

Oh.

For Maria and Ray.

Library of Congress Cataloging-in-Publication Data

Names: Wenzel, Brendan, author, illustrator.
Title: Inside Cat / Brendan Wenzel.
Description: San Francisco : Chronicle Books,
2021. | Audience: Ages 3-5. |
  Summary: Told in rhyming text, Inside Cat views
  the world through many windows, watching the
  birds, squirrels, and people go by—but when the
  door opens it discovers a whole new view.
Identifiers: LCCN 2020056859 | ISBN 9781452173191
(hardcover)
Subjects: LCSH: Cats—Juvenile fiction. | Perspective
(Philosophy)—Juvenile fiction. | Imagination—
Juvenile fiction. | Stories in rhyme. | CYAC: Stories
in rhyme. | Cats—Fiction. | Perspective (Philosophy)—
Fiction. | Windows—Fiction. | LCGFT: Stories
in rhyme. | Picture books.
Classification: LCC PZ8.3.W4653 In 2021 | DDC
  813.6 [E]—dc23
LC record available at https://lccn.loc.gov/2020056859

Manufactured in China.

MIX
Paper from
responsible sources
FSC™ C104723
FSC
www.fsc.org

Design by Jennifer Tolo Pierce.
Typeset in Miller Text.
The illustrations in this book were rendered in
a variety of media, including cut paper, colored
pencil, oil pastels, marker, and the computer.

10 9 8 7 6 5 4 3 2 1

Chronicle Books LLC
680 Second Street
San Francisco, California 94107

Chronicle Books—we see things differently. Become
part of our community at www.chroniclekids.com.